D1643068

From your Diary with Love

Don't Do Disco

On her tenth birthday, shy Evie Denham's life is turned around by a special present. In the pages of a beautiful purple diary lies the key to her happiness . . .

When her family moves from London to the little town of Crossacre, talented dancer Evie finds it difficult to settle in to her new life. On Evie's birthday, her mysterious neighbour, Mrs Volkov, gives her a beautiful purple velvet diary as a present. But this is no ordinary journal: every time Evie pens an entry and tucks it under her pillow overnight, she discovers the book has written back the following morning with words of guidance. Evie's diary soon becomes her treasured friend, holding the secret to her finding her feet in Crossacre, and giving her the confidence to do what she does best:

dance!

'These *From Your Diary With Love* books are good because they're about dancing and I love dancing a lot'
Grace, age 7

'My favourite bit in this story was when Lottie got told off because she is horrible'
Alice, age 8

'I finished this book in two days because I loved it so much'
Isobel, age 8

'I think this series is the greatest!'
Caitlin, age 9

'Really good!'
Lily, age 7

We want to hear what you think about From Your Diary With Love! *Visit*

www.egmont.co.uk/fromyourdiary

where the magic continues . . .

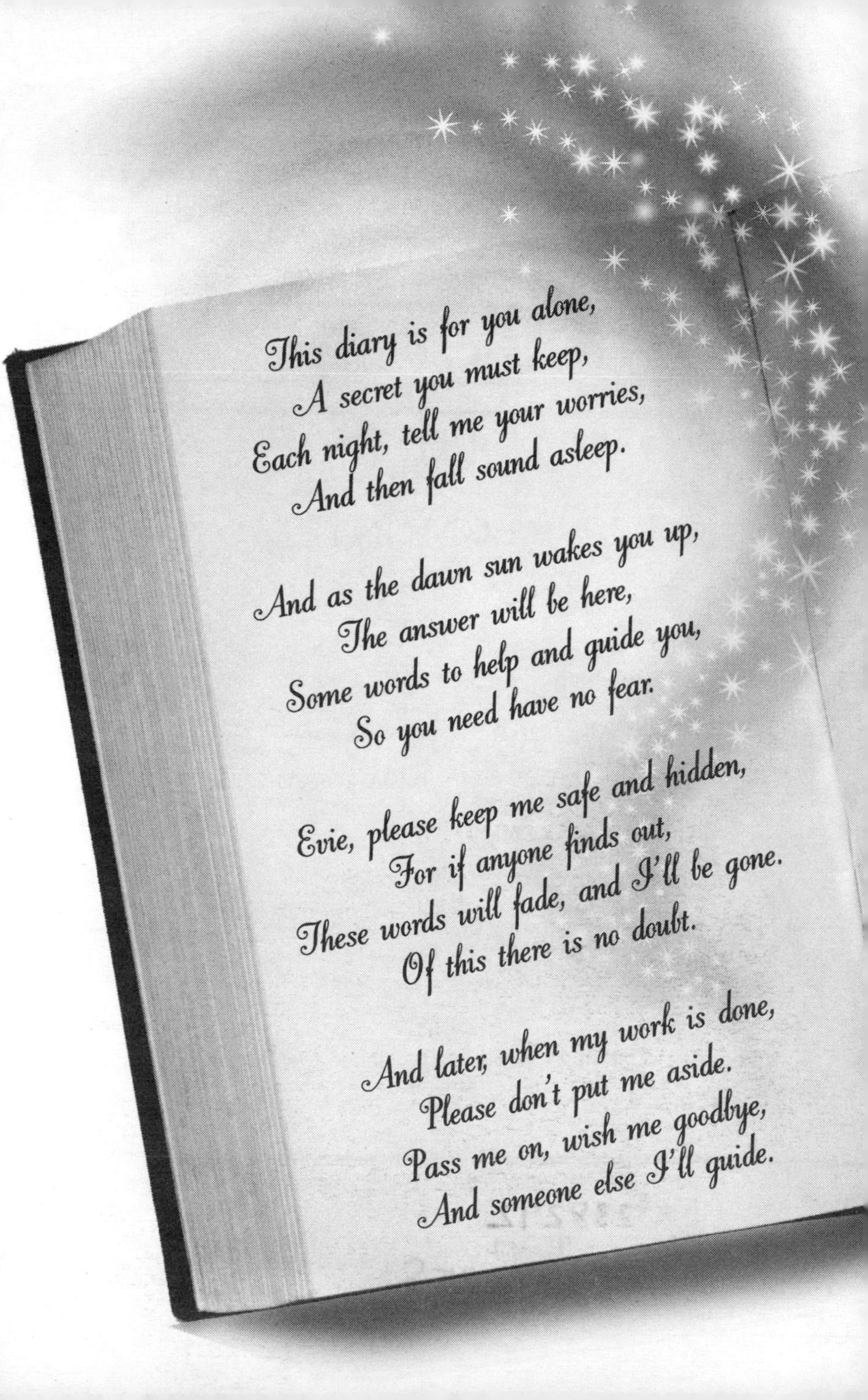

This diary is for you alone,
A secret you must keep,
Each night, tell me your worries,
And then fall sound asleep.

And as the dawn sun wakes you up,
The answer will be here,
Some words to help and guide you,
So you need have no fear.

Evie, please keep me safe and hidden,
For if anyone finds out,
These words will fade, and I'll be gone.
Of this there is no doubt.

And later, when my work is done,
Please don't put me aside.
Pass me on, wish me goodbye,
And someone else I'll guide.

Special thanks to:
Joanna Tubbs, West Jesmond Primary School, Maney Hill Primary School and Courthouse Junior School

EGMONT
We bring stories to life

Don't Do Disco first published in Great Britain 2008
by Egmont UK Limited
239 Kensington High Street, London W8 6SA

Text by Joanna Tubbs
Illustrations by Mélanie Florain

ISBN 978 1 4052 3950 9

1 3 5 7 9 10 8 6 4 2

A CIP catalogue record for this title is available from the British Library

Typeset by Avon DataSet Ltd, Bidford on Avon, Warwickshire
Printed and bound in Great Britain by the CPI Group

From Your Diary with Love

Don't Do Disco

Laura Baker

Illustrated by Mélanie Florain

EGMONT

The Denham Family

Charlie Denham

He's Evie's cool older brother who has lots of friends at school and loves playing sport, but always finds time to look out for his little sister

Evie Denham

Evie is a shy, quiet girl but with a little help and advice she hopes to make all her dancing dreams come true

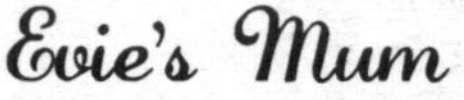

She's a nurse at the local hospital and is keen for her children to feel at home in Crossacre

Evie's Dad

He's happy to have escaped city life, and when he's not enjoying the quiet surroundings of Crossacre he's running his own Internet business

Josh Denham

He's Evie's little brother. He can be a nosy pest a lot of the time, but he loves Evie really and looks up to her a lot

The Malkova Dance Academy
Students and Staff

Dame Malkova
The legendary prima ballerina
who founded the academy
and who still manages to inspire
the students years later
Lauren
Davies
Evie's friend and
a natural athlete
Miss Connie Swann
She's a beautiful and kind
dance teacher who always
inspires her students
Matt
Shanklin
He's the only
boy at the
academy and a
reluctant dancer
Beth Dickinson
She's Evie's best
friend and excellent
at modern dance

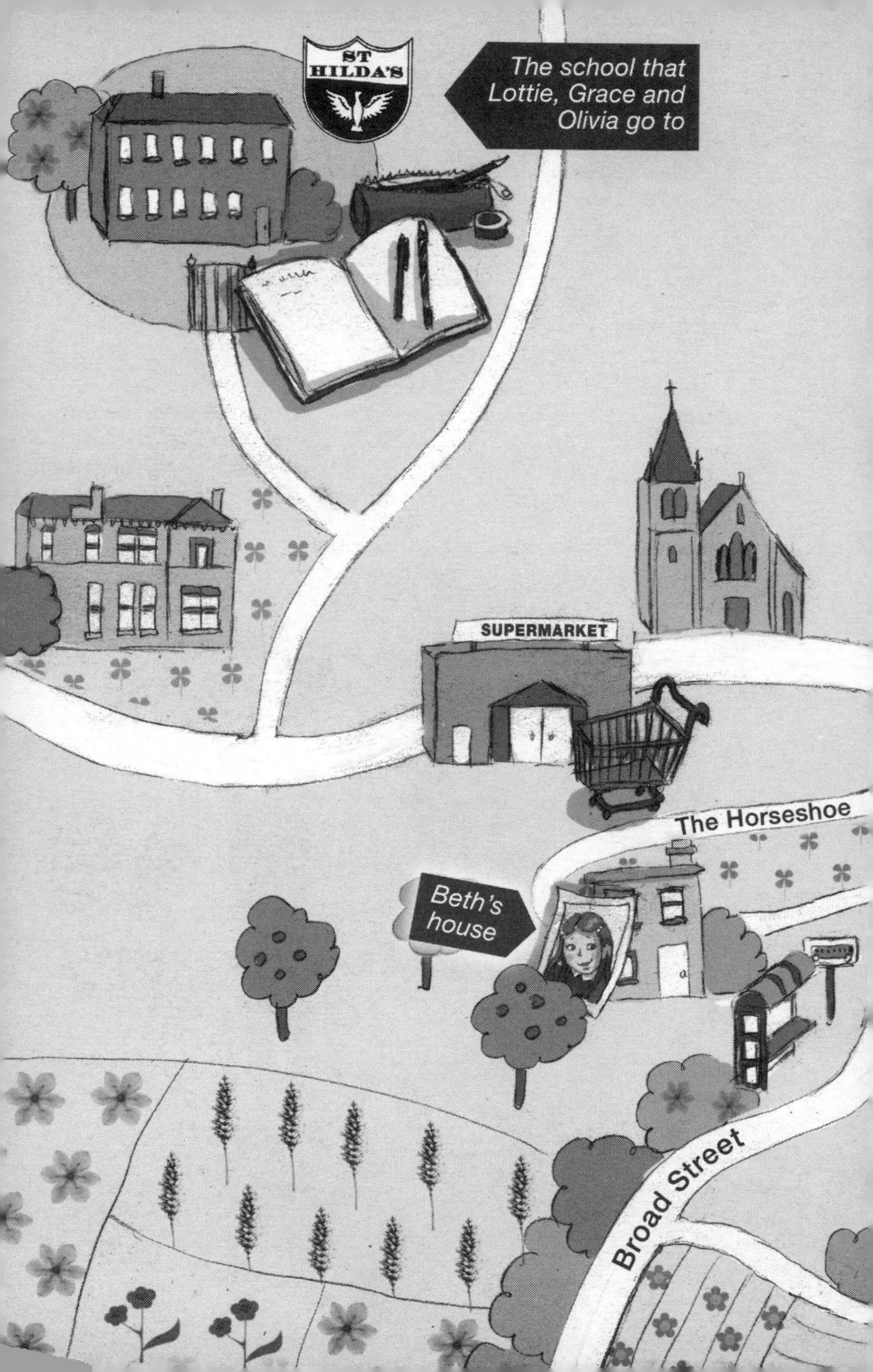
ST HILDA'S
The school that Lottie, Grace and Olivia go to
SUPERMARKET
The Horseshoe
Beth's house
Broad Street

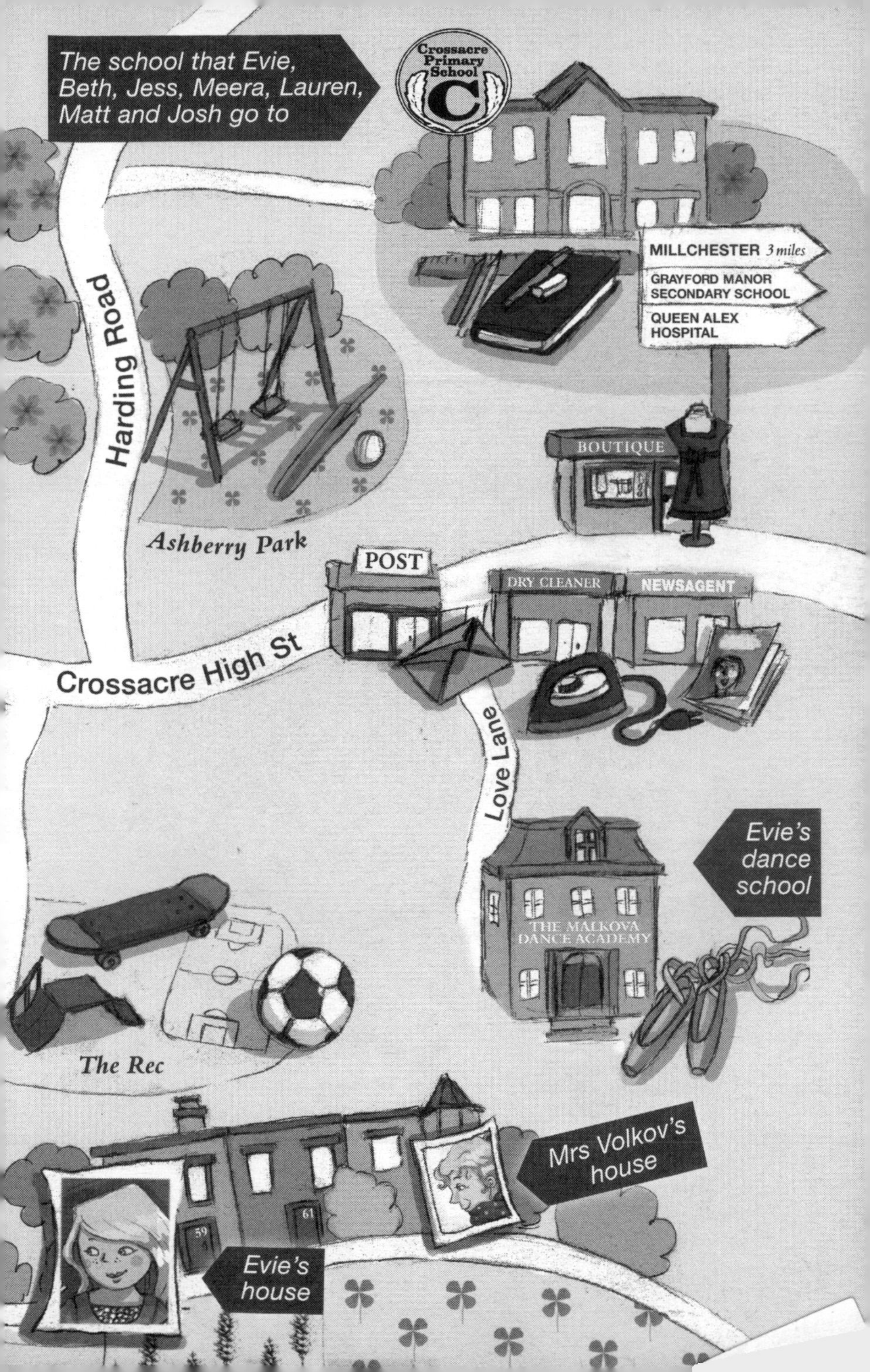
The school that Evie, Beth, Jess, Meera, Lauren, Matt and Josh go to
Crossacre Primary School
C
Harding Road
MILLCHESTER 3 miles
GRAYFORD MANOR SECONDARY SCHOOL
QUEEN ALEX HOSPITAL
BOUTIQUE
Ashberry Park
POST
DRY CLEANER
NEWSAGENT
Crossacre High St
Love Lane
Evie's dance school
THE MALKOVA DANCE ACADEMY
The Rec
Mrs Volkov's house
61
59
Evie's house

Contents

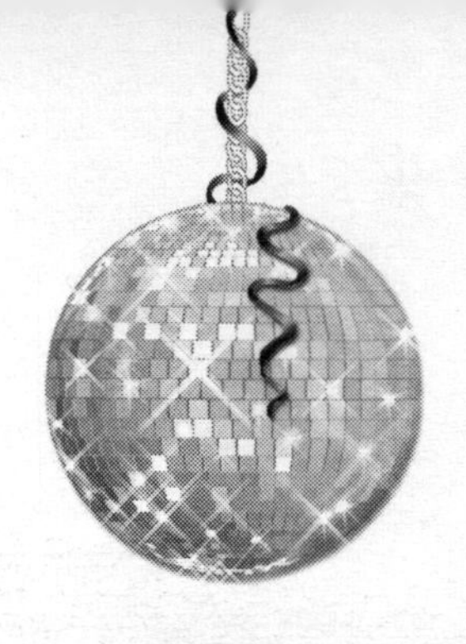

Chapter One – A Star Is Bored 1

Chapter Two – Do Doctors Dance? 10

Chapter Three – Ballet Shoes to Party Shoes 18

Chapter Four – Party Butterflies 26

Chapter Five – Tea For Three 33

Chapter Six – A Perfect Plan 41

Chapter Seven – Drawing and Drama 50

Chapter Eight – A Party of One 60

Chapter Nine – The Dress of Dreams 70

Chapter Ten – Don't Do Disco 78

Ballet facts, quizzes and a hair-do to create! 89

***Step Back In Time* Sneak Preview**

Chapter One – Sleepover Secrets 97

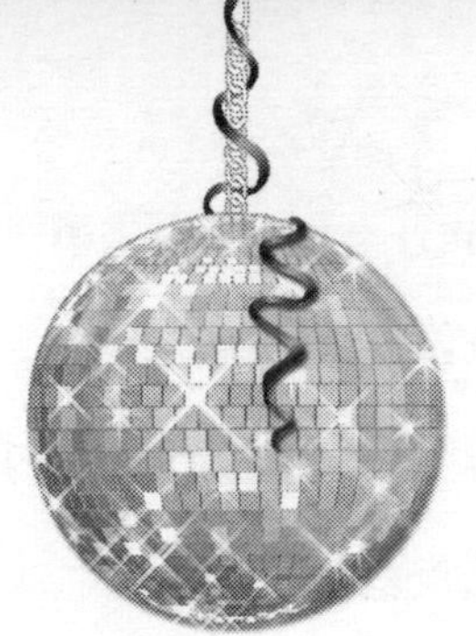

Chapter One

A Star Is Bored

'Poor Jess! Missing ballet to do extra maths,' whispered Evie as she held her arms like a halo above her head. 'It's *so* unfair!'

Miss Connie clapped. 'OK, class. Time to warm down. Breathe out slowly and gently lower your arms.'

'And on a Saturday, too!' said Meera quietly.

'Yes,' murmured Beth. 'It's loads more fun

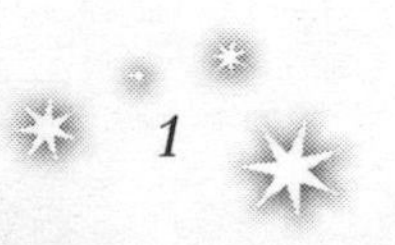

when we're all here.'

'Well done, everyone!' Miss Connie said. 'Now don't forget – jazz and modern for Wednesday's class.'

A soft patter of ballet shoes scurried across the studio floor to the changing room. Leading the way in a great rush was Matt Shanklin. He had an anxious look on his face and kept pushing his hair out of his eyes.

'Matt!' called Miss Connie. 'Lottie needs a partner to practise her duet with. Would you mind staying behind for a few minutes?'

Matt let out a groan and Evie saw his face fall with disappointment. The last thing in the *world* that he wanted to do was stay behind for extra ballet. There were so many better things to be doing on Saturday morning, like lounging on the sofa watching TV!

'Sorry, Miss Connie,' he called, running even

faster. 'I can't today. My mum's waiting for me.' He reached the boys' changing room but, just as he stretched out his hand to open the door, Mrs Shanklin's shrill voice cried out.

'Do stay and dance, Matty, darling! There's no hurry. I could wait all day if necessary!'

Evie saw Matt falter and his body sag like a party balloon that had lost its air; he shrugged

and shuffled slowly back on to the dance floor.

The same thing happened every week, but Matt never managed to avoid it.

Two years ago, Mrs Shanklin had watched a DVD and seen Billy Elliot dance his way to fame and glory: from that moment she knew that her brilliant Matty was going to be a star!

First she took him to the hairdresser for a Billy Elliot hairstyle, and then to The Malkova Dance Academy for ballet lessons.

Miss Connie was thrilled to have a boy in her class at last, and Matt found himself playing the male lead in every performance.

Mrs Shanklin thought this *proved* his brilliance! She attended every performance, cheering and clapping more than any other parent. Sometimes she even threw Matt flowers.

'May I stay and watch?' said Mrs Shanklin eagerly and, without waiting for an answer, sat on the bench.

'Poor Matt,' whispered Evie to Beth. 'Maybe he should swap with Jess – he looks like he'd *rather* be doing extra maths!'

Lottie was working for another certificate. Determined to be the best dancer in the academy, she was taking the practice *very* seriously.

Evie, Beth, Meera and Lauren thought it might be interesting and hung back to watch.

'Matt,' said Miss Connie, 'please curl your left arm above your head.'

Matt did as instructed.

'Now bend your right knee . . . just a little more. Very good, Matt.'

'Hurrah! Bravo!' yelled Mrs Shanklin, and clapped loudly.

Lottie pulled a sour face.

Miss Connie raised her eyebrows. 'Now, Lottie. If you would step this way and –'

'Oops!' muttered Matt, losing his balance and stamping on Lottie's foot.

'Owww! Careful, you idiot!' yelled Lottie.

Up jumped Mrs Shanklin. 'Don't you call my Matty names!' she shouted. 'He's a genius!'

'Poor Matt!' said Evie. 'I think we'd better leave.'

Evie spent the afternoon working on her school project – 'The History of Dance in Ancient Rome'. As she worked, she kept thinking of Matt and wondered why he looked so bothered when Miss Connie called him back.

In bed that night, snug in her pyjamas, Evie switched on her bedside lamp. She reached under her pillow and slid out the very special book with a cover of soft purple velvet – her amazing diary. She would write to it like a friend, sharing her thoughts and worries. Sometimes, when she really didn't know *what* to do, it wrote back helpful, understanding advice.

She picked up her favourite rose-scented gel pen and began to write.

Dear diary,

I had a lovely morning with Beth, Lauren and Meera at dance. It was great fun, though we all wished Jess could've been there too.

One thing today made me feel sad, though. Matt Shanklin looked really upset when he had to go back and dance with Lottie.

He's a kind, quiet boy, but his mum is SO loud!

I love Mum and Dad coming to see me dance, but if they made that much fuss I'd be so embarrassed! And he always looks bored cos there aren't any other boys for him to talk to, but I can't help that, cos I'm a girl! I just wish I could help him.

Anyway, then I did some more of my history project and in the evening we watched TV and I had ice cream with about four million sprinkles, because the top fell off the pot as I poured them on! It was brilliant!

Goodbye for now, and goodnight . . .

Chapter Two

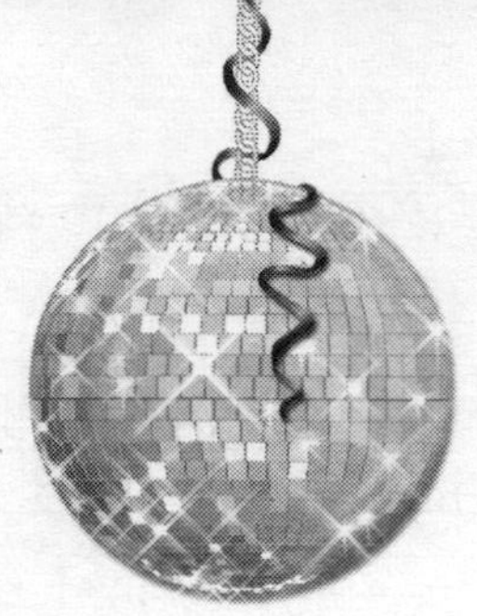

Do Doctors Dance?

Evie rested her head on her arm as she idly watched the endless grey trickles run down the classroom window. It had been raining all morning and the constant drumming of raindrops had lulled the whole class into sleepiness. Even Mr Mitchin seemed to be losing interest in the sums he had written up on the board.

'Come on, 5M, get those mathematical brains

ticking,' he said. 'I'm sure the weather will clear up by playtime and you can get some fresh air. It looks like you all need it!'

But the clouds grew heavier until it was almost dark outside. Then, with a loud crash, a fork of lightning split the sky and lit the playground brightly. Evie jumped, and the class erupted into squeals and loud chatter as the lights in the classroom flashed on and off.

'So you are all awake then!' laughed Mr Mitchin. 'It doesn't look like you lot will be going far at playtime though.'

Playtime came and Evie and her class were ushered into the library for some quiet reading. She loved to read, but the library was bursting with fidgeting children already. Evie knew it would be just her luck to end up stuck on a grubby beanbag on her own.

Then she spotted Beth and her friends waving madly at her. They were crammed around a tiny table in the corner of the library, just far enough away from the librarian to get away with some whispered gossiping. Evie grinned as she noticed that they had saved a chair for her.

'Hello!' she whispered. 'What have I missed?'

'Jess was just telling us about maths last night,' Beth said.

'Now I have to go to the maths tutor on Wednesday nights, too,' Jess explained, pulling a face. 'It's not fair! I promised Mum and Dad I would do extra maths *after* dancing, but they said it wasn't enough.'

Although Evie hadn't been friends with Jess for long, she knew that her parents wanted her to follow in their footsteps: her dad worked at Millchester General Hospital and her mum was

the doctor in Crossacre who had been so kind when Evie had earache. The girls all knew that to become a doctor you had to work very hard at school.

'I do want to do well in maths, but dancing is so much fun. I think I'd rather be a ballerina than a doctor anyway!' Jess giggled, twiddling the end of her long plait in her fingers.

Evie could tell that Jess didn't really find having a maths tutor funny at all. *I recognise that look*, she thought as she noticed Jess's mournful expression. *It's just like Matt at ballet. Dancing isn't really his dream, he's just doing it because his mum wants him to. And poor old Jess is just the same, only all she wants to do is dance!* Evie slipped her hand into her bag and ran her fingers over her diary's velvet cover. *I am so lucky to have a secret friend helping me to be the best I can be*, she thought.

Evie took hold of Jess's fiddling fingers and

squeezed her friend's hand tight.

'Want to hear some news?' she whispered, and Jess nodded furiously. 'I left my tap shoes at Malkova's and my mum popped in at the weekend to pick them up. Mum was pretty cross with me, but when she got home she said that she had had a chat with Mrs Swann. Apparently, she has got a surprise planned for the end of this half-term!'

The girls' eyes sparkled with excitement.

'What do you think it could be?' asked Jess. 'Maybe we'll get to dress up in some of Dame Malkova's old tutus.'

'Or maybe they're going to make Lottie Dean play a donkey in the next ballet show!' Beth chipped in cheekily, and the whole table burst into loud giggles.

'Erm, what's going on over there?' called the headmaster, Mr Hargreaves. 'Now, now, girls.

Can't you just sit still and read your books quietly, instead of making that almighty racket?'

Evie felt her cheeks burning brightly and wished she could disappear under the table. Everyone was looking at her! She looked across at Beth, who was biting her lip with the effort of not laughing. Evie's blushes disappeared in a second as she fought to hold back her own laughter. Lucky for them, the bell rang and the girls shoved their books into their bags before running back to the classroom.

As Evie opened her bag to put her book away, Beth caught sight of the exotic-looking purple spine of Evie's magic diary.

'Ooh, what's that purple book?' asked Beth, wide-eyed with interest.

'Oh, that. It's nothing,' replied Evie, remembering the diary's solemn words about keeping the magic a secret. 'Come on, Beth, we'd

better get a move on or we're going to end up sitting right in the front in science!'

Chapter Three

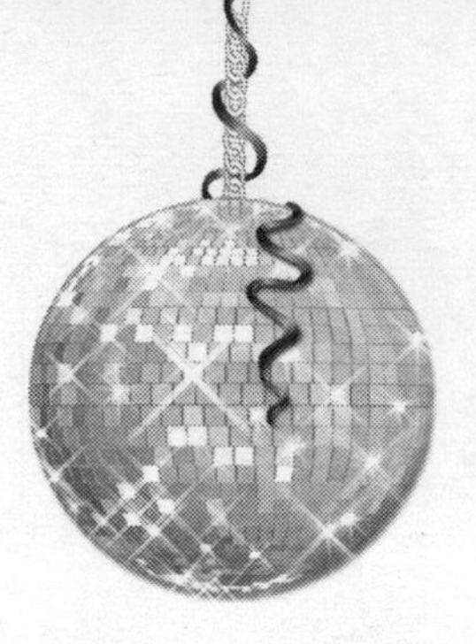

Ballet Shoes to Party Shoes

The early-morning sun shone on to Evie's pillow and gently pulled her from her dreams of twirling tutus and satin slippers. It was Saturday, Evie's favourite day of the week, and she had to get ready for her dance class. She hopped out of bed and gracefully swept around her bedroom, twisting and turning like the dancers in her dream as she collected together

the ballet clothes that were scattered across her rug. When Evie danced she could forget about being the newest girl at Crossacre Primary School and concentrate on being a real ballerina, just for a few moments.

When her ballet bag was packed, she sat on her pink rug and glimpsed a corner of her diary poking out from under her pillow. *I should definitely leave it at home today*, she thought, remembering how close Beth had come to uncovering her secret the day before at school. She pulled the diary from its hiding place and felt that familiar tingle as her fingers brushed against its rich velvet cover. Her heart pounded as she peeked inside the parchment pages to find a new message from her magical friend.

Good luck for your last dance class this half-term, Evie! As long as you point your toes, hold your head high and keep smiling, you will shine brightly.

I expect you can't wait to find out more about that surprise at Malkova's.

It does sound very exciting! I'm sure you'll find out what it is all about soon. Perhaps it's something that will help make your new friendships in Crossacre grow stronger.

Remember to keep our secret safe, Evie, or the magic will be broken.

From your diary with love.

As Evie read the final words, her bedroom door opened with a loud creak.

'Morning, Evie-weevie!' Josh screeched, almost tripping over his rumpled pyjamas. Evie sprang back into bed, clasping the book tightly under her duvet.

'What have you got there?' he asked, scrunching up his face inquisitively.

'Nothing,' said Evie.

'Then what are you hiding?' asked her brother.

'Nothing!' she said again.

'Then why is your face all red and your voice all funny?' Josh said.

'And why does your hair look so silly?' Evie replied, desperately trying to change the subject.

Her little brother rubbed both hands through his hair, making it stick up even more wildly than it had before. Evie grinned as he crossed his eyes and poked out his tongue.

Phew, she thought. But she knew that he wouldn't be distracted for long. *I'd better keep the diary with me. Keeping it secret is hard work!*

After changing into her practice leotard and cardigan, Evie wrapped her hooded top around the book and tucked it safely inside her ballet bag. The studio buzzed with excited chatter as she ran to take her place at the *barre*. Evie stretched to warm up, eager to dance her best in the last class of half-term.

'Point those toes, Beth,' Miss Connie called as the class *jeté*-ed in a circle.

The hour flew by and soon the music stopped and class was over.

'Well done, class,' said Miss Connie. 'Now, before you go and enjoy your holidays, Mrs Swann has some important news for you. You'll find out all about it in the main studio shortly.' Beth bounced up and down with excitement.

'Ooh, a surprise!' she squealed. 'I bet I can guess what it is. We're putting on another play! Or it's a party! Or we're going on an outing!'

'Come on, silly,' said Evie with a grin. 'Let's go and find out!'

The class filed through to the main studio,

chattering excitedly. They couldn't wait to find out about the surprise!

'Calm down, children,' called Mrs Swann, her clear voice carrying across the noisy studio. 'You'll all find out soon enough, if you can manage to keep quiet for a moment.'

Within a few seconds, the chatter had stopped. Despite her silvery hair, Mrs Swann still had all the grace and elegance of a young ballerina, and the pupils at Malkova's adored her.

'Once again, I'm pleased to say that I have seen a huge improvement in your dancing since the beginning of term,' she continued. 'As a reward, we are going to throw a party for everyone next week. Perhaps I will learn something about disco dancing from you all!' Mrs Swann's laughter tinkled round the studio as Evie felt a wave of butterflies in her tummy.

The students burst into applause, while ripples

of whispers about disco lights, party snacks and pop music began to pass through the crowd. A beaming Beth caught Evie's eye and winked.

I'm excited too, Evie told herself, *so why is my tummy so jumpy?*

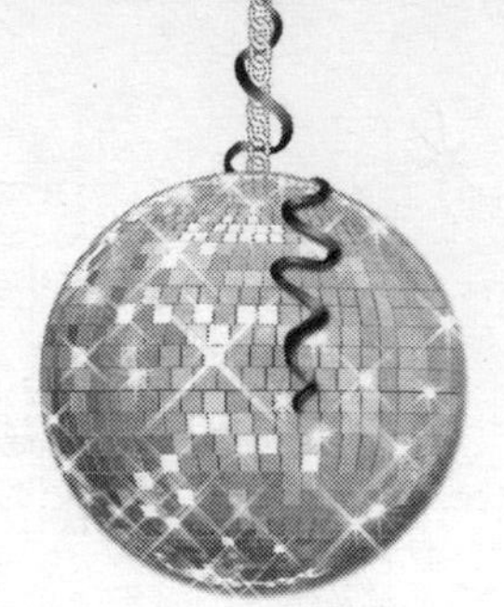

Chapter Four

Party Butterflies

Evie's mind whirred as she and the other students walked down the tree-lined path that led from Malkova's to Crossacre town square.

If only Hannah could come to the party, Evie thought, suddenly missing her best friend a lot. She pictured the two of them twirling around in the flashing lights after a whole afternoon of getting ready together.

But Hannah was miles and miles away in London, and Evie didn't know who she was going to discuss outfits, practise hairstyles or make up dance routines with. Beth and the other girls were nice, but Evie knew there was nothing like having a best friend around when it came to going to parties.

Suddenly, a loud voice brought Evie back to reality with a jolt.

'Mummy bought me the most *perfect* dress last week,' came the unmistakeable voice of Lottie Dean. 'It's cream silk with gold sequins and it will look stunning under the disco lights. I've even got a matching bag!'

Beth must have been listening too, as she rolled her eyes at Evie. Evie felt Beth's arm wrap around her own, and the two girls skipped ahead to catch up with Matt.

'Matt! Isn't it brilliant news about the party?' Beth said breathlessly.

'I suppose so,' he replied.

'You don't sound too sure,' Evie said, recognising her own feelings in his tone.

'It's just . . . sometimes I get a bit fed up of being the only boy,' he admitted with a sheepish half-smile. 'I'm not sure how much fun the disco will be if I'm surrounded by girls!'

'Fair enough,' said Beth. 'I'm not sure I'd like to be surrounded by boys, either! Hey, Evie, can you imagine going to a party where you were the *only girl*?!'

'Yuck!' shuddered Evie, feeling even more sorry for Matt.

'Hello, pretty boy,' came a voice from behind a tree.

They turned a corner and came face-to-face with a bunch of boys from 5M.

'Oh, great,' muttered Matt, who looked as though he wanted the ground to swallow him up.

Anthony and Joseph, the class jokers, were standing in the middle of the path twirling clumsy pirouettes and falling about laughing.

'Nice legs!' jeered a boy in a black beanie, pointing at Matt's shiny blue tights.

Evie desperately wanted to stand up for him but felt far too shy to speak out in front of all those boys. All she could manage was to shoot them what she hoped was a fierce face while searching desperately for something smart to say.

'We haven't forgotten the time you all dressed up as flowers for the school play in year one, boys!' said Beth, her eyes sparkling mischievously. 'You all wore petals around your ikkle faces. So *pretty*!' Beth always had an answer ready and was never afraid to stand up to the boys. They shut up immediately.

'Thanks, Beth,' Matt said gratefully as he walked to meet his mum. She was in the car honking her horn loudly and impatiently.

'Mattie, darling!' she called from the car window. 'Do hurry, I want to hear all about ballet. Did you point your toes like I told you?' Matt studied his feet as he shuffled to the car.

'Poor Matt,' Beth said to Evie as they waited by the Post Office to be collected.

'I know,' agreed Evie. 'It's so unfair. It's not his fault that his mum makes him wear those tights.' Then, something green and sparkly caught her eye. It was a beautiful sequinned dress that was hanging in the window of *The Boutique*, a shop next door to the Post Office.

'Hey, look at that dress!' Evie said to Beth.

'Gorgeous!' said Beth. 'That would look great

on you!' Just for a second, Evie caught a glimpse of herself dancing in the green dress under flashing disco lights. *Maybe I am looking forward to the disco, after all*, she thought.

Chapter Five

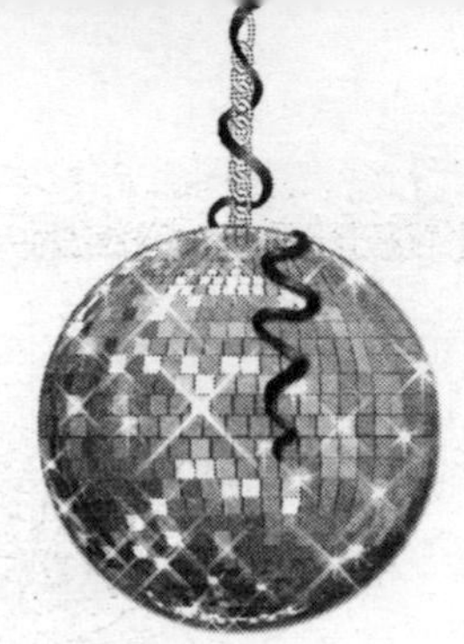

Tea For Three

'Muuuuum! Charlie just finished up the chocolate sauce! It's not fair,' pouted Josh, as his older brother poured the last drops of warm chocolate sauce over an enormous bowl of ice cream.

'Charlie, share that with your brother, please. You've had so much food already today, you'll burst!' said Mrs Denham.

The kitchen table was covered with the remains of Sunday lunch and Evie felt full and sleepy.

'Do we have to wash up?' asked Evie, with one eye on the back door.

Her mum laughed gently and said, 'No, off you go. I'd escape from those mad brothers while you can if I were you!'

Evie picked up her bag, then snuck out of the back door before her brothers even noticed that she had moved. She followed the winding path into her favourite part of the garden. It was a secret spot, sheltered from the noise of the house and the heat of the sun by an old, leafy tree.

Evie's drowsiness vanished as she pulled her diary from her bag and felt its weight in her hands. Curling up on the bench, surrounded by the sweet smell of the roses that coiled around the tree's ancient trunk, she opened the diary. Once again, the page that followed her last entry was covered in curly handwriting:

Evie, please don't worry about the disco. Your friendships in Crossacre are growing stronger every day so you can't fail to have fun. You might think that

you didn't help Matt, but he was very pleased to have a friend like you on his side. And perhaps there is another way that you could make things easier for him. If only the other children knew what a special place Malkova's is, they probably wouldn't tease Matt about going to dance lessons.

Finally, what you wear isn't too important. You would still shine even in your oldest dress. It's nice to get dressed up though, and maybe you will find something extra special that will make you feel like the belle of the ball.

From your diary with love.

Evie closed the diary and hugged it to herself. She felt so lucky to have it. However worried she was feeling, reading her diary always seemed to make her feel better. *I wonder what my diary meant by there being another way of helping Matt?* she thought. *I can't imagine ever convincing Anthony and Joseph to come along to Malkova's!* Then, Evie had a thought. Maybe the boys *could* be convinced if there was a disco involved! She pictured it in her mind: lots of food, dancing and flashing lights. They would love it! *It's the perfect solution*, thought Evie. Matt would be pleased if some boys were invited, Mrs Swann could find some new dancers and perhaps the party would be the best that Crossacre had ever seen. There was just one problem: how on earth could she get in touch with Mrs Swann?

Evie leaned back against the bench to try and work out a plan. In the distance, she could hear voices and the tinkling of china. Curious, Evie stood up on the bench's seat and peeped over the ivy-covered fence behind it.

To her amazement, she saw Mrs Swann sitting on Mrs Volkov's patio two gardens away. Both ladies were drinking tea, their cups and saucers chinking as they chatted together. Mrs Volkov turned around and looked Evie straight in the eye.

Oh, dear, thought Evie as she felt a warm blush spread across her face. *I've been caught out now!*

But, instead of telling Evie off for peeking, Mrs Volkov simply smiled. She didn't seem at all surprised to see Evie's face pop over the fence like that. In fact, she beckoned for her to come and join them. *How strange,* thought Evie as she climbed down from the bench.

'Mum, can I go and have tea with Mrs Volkov?' Evie called, her voice quavering with nerves.

'Of course,' Mrs Denham replied.

Evie unlatched the tall gate at the end of the garden and walked along the overgrown path that led to number 63, where Mrs Volkov was already waiting.

'Come in, dear,' she said kindly. Evie felt nervous and a little confused as she noticed that there was already an extra cup of tea on the table. It was as if they had both been waiting for her to arrive. 'Take a seat and tell us how you are.'

'You look lost in thought, Evie,' said Mrs Swann. 'What are you thinking about?'

Evie's cup wobbled in its saucer as she picked it up with shaking hands.

'Well, um, I just thought . . .' Evie began. She felt a little odd sitting in the garden with Malkova's elegant principal and the mysterious old lady who had passed on the magical diary.

'Go on, dear,' said Mrs Swann.

'M-m-maybe we could invite everyone in Crossacre School to the disco, not just the dance pupils,' Evie blurted out, her cheeks burning red hot. The ladies looked at each other and smiled.

I think they like the idea! Evie thought, hugging herself.

The disco was looking better than ever!

Chapter Six

A Perfect Plan

'What an excellent idea!' said Mrs Swann, clasping her hands together with glee. 'Wouldn't it be wonderful if we were able to find some new dancers for Malkova's? It's the perfect opportunity to show the youngsters of Crossacre exactly what goes on at the academy. And if we're lucky enough to find some more pupils who are anything like you, Evie, that will be

a wonderful thing.'

Evie beamed with pride. It had certainly been worth overcoming those butterflies to explain her idea to Mrs Swann.

Mrs Volkov looked over at Evie, her eyes twinkling happily.

'You might be able to raise some extra pennies, too,' the snowy-haired lady added.

'Oh, yes! Now, we just have to think of a way

of encouraging all of these lovely young people to come along,' said Mrs Swann. Evie looked down at her hands, which were covered in bright pen marks from some drawing she had been doing earlier.

'How about a competition to draw a poster telling everyone all about the party?' Evie suggested.

'Perfect!' said Mrs Swann. 'We could make copies of the winning entry and post it around Crossacre to make sure that everyone knows all about it. I'll go and type up a newsletter right away,' Mrs Swann added, picking up her brown leather handbag from under the garden table. 'Every house in Crossacre will have a copy by tomorrow afternoon.'

And with that, she walked down the garden path, her steps as dainty as a fairy's.

'Well done, Evie,' said Mrs Volkov, her eyes crinkling at the corners as she smiled warmly.

'Your idea is such a kind one, and I know that Matt will be pleased that you thought of such a nice way of helping him.'

Evie felt so happy that she thought she might burst. Mrs Swann and Mrs Volkov were proud of her, she had found a way to help Matt and the plans for the disco were getting bigger and better by the minute.

'Thank you, Mrs Volkov,' she called as she let herself out of the back gate and followed the path back to her own house.

Evie tried to picture herself at the disco but all that she could see was a crowd of unfamiliar faces. Although she knew it could be a great chance to make some new friends, it seemed daunting.

I know I'll miss Hannah, but at least Beth will be there, she thought. She couldn't wait to tell her newest friend all about her strange afternoon!

'Mum!' she called as she opened the back door. 'Can I phone Beth, please?'

'Of course, love,' her mum replied, as Evie tapped Beth's number into the phone.

'Hiya, Beth, it's Evie,' she said, as her friend answered. 'I've got some news! You know the disco at Malkova's? Everyone from school is going to be invited too!'

'Everyone?' gasped Beth. 'Wow! It's going to be amazing!'

Evie told Beth about the poster competition and having tea with Mrs Swann and Mrs Volkov. There was something about the afternoon that she couldn't quite explain – a sort of magic that she felt in the air when Mrs Volkov was around – but Evie pushed the thought to the back of her mind and the pair continued to gossip about the party instead. Beth was crazy about dancing and an invitation to a huge disco was her dream come true! Evie felt lucky to have such a lively friend to go to the party with.

'So what about this poster competition then?' said Evie. 'Shall we enter?' Evie knew that Beth loved drawing, even if she wasn't quite as good as Meera.

'Definitely!' her friend replied, excitedly. 'Why don't you come over tomorrow after school and we can get started? Mum says you're welcome.'

'Excellent plan!' said Evie. 'Mum, can I go to Beth's tomorrow, please?'

'Yes, darling, as long as that's OK with Beth's mum,' said Mrs Denham, who was making a pot of tea.

'It's all settled then,' said Beth, overhearing what Mrs Denham had said. 'Don't forget your pens!'

'That all sounded very exciting,' said Mrs Denham, wiping her hands on her stripy apron. 'A disco, hey? And tea at Beth's house tomorrow after school. What a lot of fun you're having these days!' Evie grinned. 'How about we go shopping for something new for you to wear to this disco?'

Evie turned to her mum, her eyes shining. 'Really?' she said. 'That would be brilliant!'

'You want to feel sparkly and pretty on your big day,' said Mrs Denham as she wrapped Evie up in a huge cuddle.

A lovely warmth spread through Evie as she dashed upstairs to find her diary soon after. She had so much news to share! She pulled it out from under her pillow, grabbed her rose-scented gel pen and began to write:

Dear diary,

What a day! I don't know where to start. Mum made a delicious roast, then afterwards I overheard Mrs Swann and Mrs Volkov chatting in the garden. I thought they might tell me off for being nosy, but Mrs Volkov invited me round for tea instead! It was the perfect chance to tell her about my idea. You see, I had been thinking that it would be great if we could invite everyone from Crossacre to the disco.

I didn't need to be nervous – they loved the idea! Mrs Swann even said we can have a competition to design a disco poster, and I'm going to Beth's tomorrow so we can make ours together.

I'm feeling less and less nervous about the disco, and more and more excited about making new friends in Crossacre. Maybe I will like it here, after all.

Oh, I'm so sleepy! Thank you again for writing to me.

Love, Evie.

PS – I nearly forgot. Mum said I could get a new

dress for the disco! I wonder if that green dress is still hanging in the window in town . . .

With heavy eyes, Evie slipped the diary back under the pillow and turned off her lamp. It was only as she drifted off to sleep that she started to think back over what Mrs Volkov had said about Matt. Evie didn't think the old lady had ever met him, so how could she possibly have known what he had got to do with any of it, she wondered dozily.

Chapter Seven

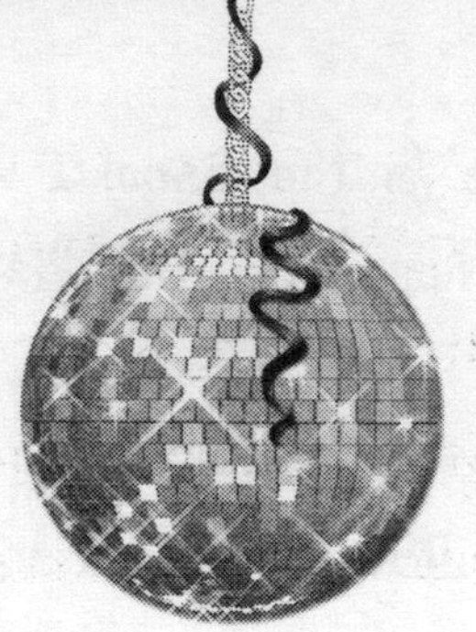

Drawing and Drama

'Cooee!' Beth shouted through the letterbox in her front door. 'It's me and Evie, Mum!'

'Come on in, girls,' said Mrs Dickinson, who had rosy cheeks and long brown hair just like Beth. 'The Malkova's newsletter came through the door today. It said your posters have to be finished by Wednesday.'

Wednesday?! That was only two days away!

The girls dashed into the dining room where Evie got her best pens out of her bag and Beth tipped a box of pencils, crayons and glitter glue on to the table with a clatter. They settled down, each with a fresh piece of white paper.

Beth drew some bold lines across the page with a thick red felt tip, while Evie thoughtfully nibbled the end of a pencil, waiting for an idea to pop into her head.

'I just can't wait!' said Beth, grinning excitedly as her poster took shape.

'I know, it's going to be sooo brilliant!' agreed Evie, lightly sketching the outline of a dancer on to the paper. 'Are you any good at disco dancing?'

'Yeah!' Beth said, nodding enthusiastically. 'I mean, I'm not as good as Lottie Dean, obviously,' she added, rolling her eyes. 'But Miss Connie showed us a few moves last term and it was so much fun.'

'We should make up a routine,' suggested Evie.

'Good idea!' said Beth, vigorously colouring in some bright green stars.

'Do you think the St Hilda's lot will be the same as they are in dance class?' asked Evie.

'What, show-offs, you mean?' said Beth, with a twinkle in her eye. 'I should think so! But we won't let them spoil our fun. Tomorrow, let's get

started on the best disco dance routine Crossacre has ever seen!' The girls began to plan a few moves and soon their pens had been forgotten in favour of high kicks and hand jives.

'Hold on . . .' said Evie suddenly. 'Do you think Jess will even be allowed to come to the disco? Her parents are so strict.'

'I know,' said Beth sadly. 'I hope so. It wouldn't

be the same without her. And I reckon it's quite important for a doctor to be able to disco dance!'

'If you say so!' said Evie, with a giggle. Her poster, a ballerina dancing in front of disco lights, was looking pretty good. Beth suddenly burst into a fit of laughter, spilling glitter all over her bright poster.

'Can you imagine Anthony and Joseph dancing?' Beth said, barely able to get her words out between chuckles.

She jumped down from her chair and did an impression that looked a bit like someone frantically escaping a swarm of bees. She flopped on the floor and wriggled about pulling crazy faces until tears of laughter were streaming down both girls' cheeks.

Still giggling, Beth hauled herself back on to her chair and began to add a touch more glitter glue to her wild-looking poster, while Evie added some sparkles to a disco ball that she had drawn above her dancer's head. Before long, they were both absorbed in their work again, Beth idly kicking her foot against the chair leg.

'Oh, sorry, Evie,' said Beth, as she accidentally knocked over Evie's bag.

As she bent down to pick it up, Evie sprang to her feet and grabbed her diary, which was lying under the chair.

'What *is* that?' asked Beth, intrigued by the mystical-looking purple book that her friend was so protective about.

'Oh, nothing,' said Evie, aware of how unconvincing she sounded.

'Can I see it then?' asked Beth.

Evie felt a warm pink blush ri[illegible]ks.

'Um, it's just a sketchbook,' [illegible]

pictures aren't that good.'

'Oh, go on,' pleaded Be[illegible]

Evie heard her diary's solemn promise ring through her head:

Please, Evie, keep me hidden,
For if anyone finds out,
These words will fade, and I'll be gone.
Of this there is no doubt.

'Really, it's nothing interesting, it doesn't matter,' said Evie, who knew she had to protect her diary's secret, however silly it made her sound.

'I don't understand,' said Beth, hurt. 'I thought we were friends, and friends don't keep secrets from each other.'

Evie felt terrible but she couldn't imagine losing her diary's magic now. She shrugged her

shoulders and twiddled her pencil unhappily.

'Fine,' said Beth, pressing her lips together. 'If you won't share with me, then I won't share with you.' She scooped a higgledy-piggledy pile of pens towards her side of the table and carried on colouring without a word.

Evie felt muddled up inside. *I wouldn't like it if Beth or Hannah kept secrets from me*, she thought. *But what else am I supposed to do?*

She was shaken from her gloomy thoughts as Beth's mum brought a tray with two glasses of fruit smoothies and a plate of brownies on it into the dining room.

'It sounded like feeding time in the zoo in here!' she said cheerily. 'Anyone fancy a little treat?' Evie looked across to Beth, who was staring hard at her poster. 'Is everything all right, girls?' she asked.

'Yes, Mum,' said Beth crossly. 'We're fine.'

Evie felt hollow inside and knew that she would not be able to manage a brownie or a sip of smoothie. In fact, she felt as if she couldn't even manage to finish off her colouring.

'I think I'd better go, Beth,' she said, packing up her pens. 'My mum will be expecting me.'

Tears pricking her eyes, Evie grabbed her bag and walked out. Beth barely mumbled as she left.

It was only halfway down the road that Evie remembered her poster, lying unfinished on Beth's table.

Chapter Eight

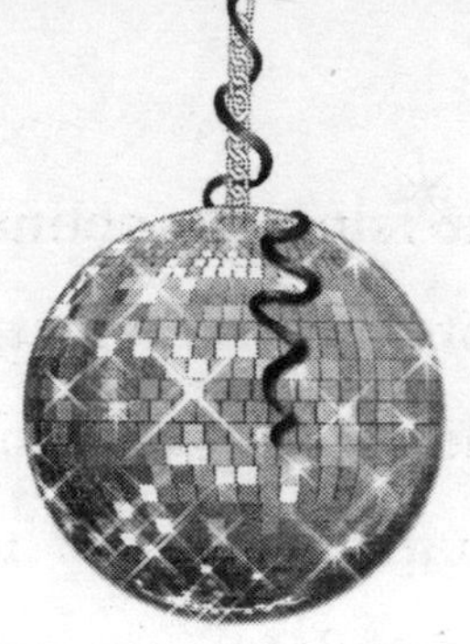

A Party of One

It looked like the party had already started as Evie approached Malkova's studio on Thursday. The happy babble of voices poured through the open windows as dance students and their parents dashed around inside, hanging banners and blowing up balloons. Evie slipped through the main door quietly. She desperately wanted to help with the disco preparations, but she was anxious about seeing Beth.

It had been a lonely few days at school. The girls hadn't been horrible to her exactly, but it had just seemed easier for Evie to fall back into the role of the new girl again. Her argument with Beth had left her with no one to speak to except her diary, and Evie just wanted to forget that it had ever happened.

She picked her way around a tangle of fairy lights, scanning the room for Beth and the others. Gazing up to the stage, she spotted her friends – if she could still call them friends – trying to pin up a huge banner.

Evie stood to one side of the stage and listened. They were all extra excited as they chatted about Jess's parents saying that she could come to the disco, after all.

'Try it a bit higher, Meera,' Miss Connie shouted up to them, her golden bun beginning to uncoil. 'But be careful on that chair – you're looking a bit wobbly!'

The girls burst into giggles as Meera dropped her end of the banner in a heap, while Miss Connie turned to Evie. 'Evie! It's lovely to see you. Can you just hop up there and help Meera, please?'

But at the mention of Evie's name, the giggles on the stage stopped. Beth caught Evie's eye, and Evie attempted a small smile. But Beth just turned away, fiddling with a piece of string.

The silence went on and on, and it was clear to everyone that Beth wasn't ready to forget about the argument just yet.

Evie looked down at her fingernails, which blurred as her eyes filled with tears. She bit her lip, determined not to cry in front of everyone. She felt a warm hand on her back.

'Come on, Evie, I've got the perfect job for

you,' said Miss Connie, steering her towards a balloon-filled corner of the studio. 'Mrs Shanklin, I've got another balloon blower for you here,' Miss Connie said, introducing Evie to Matt's mum and her troop of puffed-out volunteers. There must have been a hundred balloons bobbing around their feet already, but Mrs Shanklin didn't miss a beat.

'Perfect!' she trilled, thrusting a green balloon at Evie. 'Come on, everyone, keep blowing!'

Matt peered out from behind his mum's back, raised his eyebrows and grinned at Evie. For once, his mum's loud and bossy behaviour didn't seem to bother him. Evie had overheard him discussing the disco with some of the other boys at school. Now that the whole town was invited, Malkova's disco had become the talk of the playground.

'You coming tomorrow then, Evie?' Matt asked between puffs.

'I suppose so,' she replied, pushing back her recent tears.

'It's going to be brilliant! Nearly everyone from 5M is coming, even Anthony and Joseph!' Matt said. Evie had seen Anthony and Joseph pirouetting around Matt in the cloakroom lots of times before, teasing him for being a 'dancing sissy'. Matt couldn't hide how pleased he was that they had been won round to the idea of Malkova's.

'I don't know whose idea it was to invite everyone, but it was a great one!' Evie blushed and smiled shyly. 'Was it *you*?' Matt asked with surprise. She nodded. 'Wow!' Matt said, impressed. 'Thanks a million, Evie! This is going to be the best party ever!'

Evie slipped her hand into her bag and fondly stroked her diary's velvet cover. She was happy that the party plans had worked out for Matt,

and felt so lucky to have a secret friend at her side too.

Still puffing into a long yellow balloon, Matt's face wrinkled with concern. 'What's up, Evie?' he asked. 'Why isn't Beth talking to you?'

Evie ignored the lump in her throat and said, 'I, um, I'm not sure.' She couldn't tell Matt about her magic diary, either. He'd probably think she was bonkers! 'We just had a little argument. I hope we can be friends again.'

'Oh, I'm sure she'll forget about it all soon,' Matt said reassuringly. 'I've known Beth since nursery and her bad moods never last long. It'll all be over by the disco.' Evie smiled weakly.

'I hope so,' she said. And she really, really meant it.

'Boys and girls,' called Mrs Swann from the stage. 'What a wonderful job you have done!'

The studio had been transformed into a party paradise! Disco lights flashed and a mirrored disco ball hung above the stage. Tables covered with colourful paper tablecloths ran down one side of the room, waiting to be piled with snacks, and bunches of balloons brightened every corner.

'There's just one more thing we need to do before the disco,' Mrs Swann reminded them all, 'and that's announce the winner of the poster competition!' Murmurs and whispers passed through the crowd. Most people had seen the brightly coloured posters that had appeared all around Crossacre at the beginning of the week. The posters were beautifully drawn, but they had no name on them and everyone was anxious to find out who the artist was. 'And the winner is . . . Grace Compton!'

Mrs Swann held up a poster featuring a drawing of a disco-dancing girl and boy who looked like they were straight from the film *Grease*.

Lottie Dean and Olivia Taylor squealed with excitement and hugged their friend Grace.

Realising that all eyes were on their crowd, Lottie looked around smugly as everyone clapped. *Anyone would have thought she'd drawn it herself!* thought Evie, who was pretty impressed with Grace's drawing.

'Well done, Grace,' said Mrs Swann, presenting

her with a box of chocolates wrapped in satin ribbons.

Evie looked at her watch, glad that it was time to meet Dad and go home at last. While the others joked around and discussed disco outfits, Evie slipped out of Malkova's as quietly as she had arrived. All she wanted to do was curl up in bed with her diary and forget all about everything else.

Chapter Nine

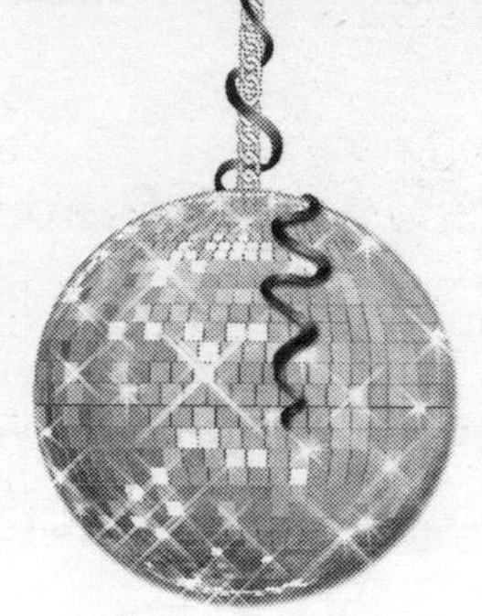

The Dress of Dreams

Evie reached out from under her snug spotted duvet and scrabbled around for the 'off' switch on her blaring alarm clock. Bleary-eyed, she knocked her bedside lamp over and sent the clock clattering to the floor.

'Ugh!' she grunted, turning to face the wall and hiding her head under the duvet. *I can't face another day of Beth's silent treatment*, she thought, squeezing her eyes shut and pretending that today wasn't happening.

After ten minutes of fitful dozing, a heavy, squealing object dived on to Evie's sleepy body.

'Wake up, Evie-weevie!' shouted Josh, bouncing up and down and patting his sister's tousled head.

'Josh! Get off!' murmured Evie as she fought off the wriggling bundle. Josh carried on poking and prodding her until she was wide awake.

'What did I do to deserve a little brother like you?!' she asked in despair, as Josh leaped around her bedroom. 'OK, you asked for it . . .' she said, grabbing him and tickling him until he was screaming with laughter.

'No, Evie!' he gasped in between giggles. 'Please . . . no . . . more . . . tickles!' He writhed out of her grasp and ran out of the bedroom, slamming the door behind him.

Peace at last, thought Evie as she curled up under her still-warm duvet. As she lay her gloomy head back on the pillow, she felt an electric prickle on the back of her neck. *My diary!* she thought. *Maybe it can tell me something that might brighten up my day.*

Dear Evie,

I'm sorry to hear that you haven't

made up with Beth and I'm not surprised that going to a party is the last thing on your mind. Life might seem tough at the moment, but if you keep your chin up and wear a smile, everything will seem better. Muster up some courage and go along to the disco. A fun evening with friends could be just what you need to make you sparkle, outside and in.

From your diary with love.

Evie closed the parchment pages feeling confused. *Sparkle, outside and in*, she thought, the words full of promise. How on earth could a dress make a difference? She knew that her friends would not judge her by what she wore, whether they were speaking to her or not. But Mum had offered to buy her a new outfit – in fact, they were due to visit Millchester after school – so there would be no harm in stopping off at *The Boutique* on the way.

Evie knew by now that it was best to trust her diary, even though its advice was sometimes strange. Its enchanted words always spoke the truth. With a glimmer of hope in her heart, Evie got ready for school, knowing that her diary's words would help her through the day.

After school, Evie and Josh piled into the car where Charlie and their mum were already waiting.

'Looking forward to getting a new dress, love?' Mum said to Evie, who was wrestling for space with Josh.

'Yes!' said Evie. 'Mum, can we stop off in Crossacre first? I saw a pretty dress in the shop by the Post Office a few days ago.'

'Of course!' said Mrs Denham. But as the car drew up outside *The Boutique*, Evie's face fell. The dress was gone! Without it, the diary's message might not come true and the disco could be a disaster after all. Mrs Denham persuaded Evie to go inside anyway.

'You never know, they might have another one tucked away somewhere,' she said, seeing Evie's disappointed face.

'Hello, we're looking for a party dress,' she said, smiling at the lady in the shop. 'My daughter saw something in the window last week. Go on, Evie, tell the lady what it was like.'

'It's green –' Evie started.

'– with a floaty skirt and sequins,' said the shop lady. 'I know just the one.' And, in a twinkle, she vanished through a silky curtain behind the till, reappearing a second later with a dress in Evie's

size. 'It's the last one in the shop. Would you like to try it on?'

Evie nodded.

She took the beautiful dress into the changing room, its delicate emerald fabric studded with sequins and finished with a butterfly-clasp belt. She felt a tingle of anticipation in her fingers as she fastened the zip, willing the dress to fit.

'Oh, love,' gasped Mum as Evie stepped into the shop. 'It fits like a dream. You look gorgeous!' Evie beamed and took a twirl. 'And it's not too dear, either,' added Mum, with a glance at the price tag.

Even Charlie, who usually couldn't care less about dresses, gave her a nod of approval.

'Would you like it, Evie?' asked Mrs Denham.

Evie hugged herself and nodded, feeling the delicate fabric move through her fingers like water. She went and changed back into her school uniform quickly while her party dress was wrapped in tissue paper.

'Thank you, Mum,' she said, carrying the smart paper bag out of the shop.

'It looks like it could have been made for you,' said Mrs Denham.

There was no doubt about it – there was something special about this dress.

Chapter Ten

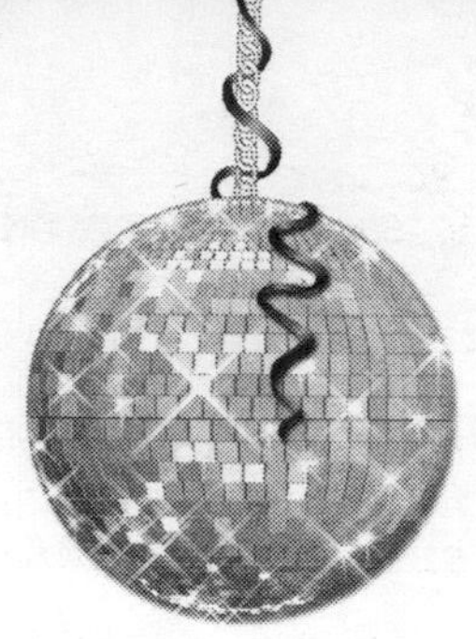

Don't Do Disco

The tissue paper rustled as Evie unwrapped and stepped into her jewelled dress later that evening. The bodice fitted snugly, the straps were just the right length and the special sequinned ballet pumps that she already had were the perfect finishing touch.

Evie looked at herself in her mum's long mirror and knew she looked ready for the party. So why did she feel so churned up inside?

I can't believe I haven't patched things up with Beth yet! she thought.

Everything at school had settled into an awkward routine: Beth totally ignored Evie, and the other girls followed her lead. Meanwhile, Evie tried desperately to blend into the shadows so no one else would notice what was going on. Right now, she just wanted to shout, 'I'm not going to the party!' and watch a DVD with her brothers. But a last twirl in the mirror reminded Evie of the diary's advice that everything would be just fine.

'Evie, it's time to go,' Mr Denham called up the stairs. Mum fussed around her at the front door and Evie tried her best to seem excited. But when her dad dropped her off at Malkova's, she had never felt so lonely.

Evie hung back as a noisy group of lads from 5M bounded along the path to Malkova's. They were joking and shouting, full of the excitement that Evie lacked. She noticed that Matt was in the middle of the crowd, looking more enthusiastic than he ever did when he was at the academy for lessons. They piled into the balloon-filled foyer, their voices fading as the door shut behind them. Evie took a deep breath and braced herself to go in – alone.

'Hi, Evie,' she heard, and looking up, saw that it was Matt. 'Are you all right?' Evie nodded, smiling weakly. 'Come on,' he said, grinning and grabbing her arm. 'It's a party – it's supposed to be fun!'

Together, they walked into Malkova's.

The studio was unrecognisable. Lines of children danced while giggling gaggles filled the corners of the room. Evie's eyes swept the room, searching for Beth, Jess, Meera and Lauren. But they were nowhere to be seen.

'Thanks for coming in with me, Matt,' she said gratefully.

'No worries. Now go and enjoy the disco,' Matt replied. 'Hey, Toby!' he shouted, running over to meet a friend.

Evie stood, self-conscious and alone, before heading to the tables piled with party food. *At least I'll look like I'm doing something other than standing round on my own*, she thought, even though she knew she couldn't eat a thing. She popped an egg mayonnaise roll and a fairy cake on to a plate and sipped from a plastic cup of orange squash.

Staring at her shoes, she walked towards the studio door when suddenly – crash! Evie fell face first into a silky cream-coloured dress, smashing her egg roll into a mess of crumbs and slopping squash all over a pair of beaded slippers.

'Oh, no! I'm so sorry,' she cried, her eyes

travelling upwards to meet the furious face of Lottie Dean.

'What have you *done*?' she shouted, as Evie noticed the squashed ham sandwich and chocolate cake that were smeared over her own emerald-green dress. 'Do you know how much this dress cost?' yelled Lottie. 'It was an absolute fortune! My mother will be furious with you!'

'Oh, dear!' cried Miss Connie, running to the rescue with a handful of wet paper towels. Evie helped her to blot the stains on Lottie's dress.

'You're making it worse!' howled Lottie. She pulled out a pink mobile phone and made a call. 'Mummy, you'll never guess what has happened.

Evie Denham has spilled squash and all sorts over my dress. It's completely ruined! I need a new outfit – now!'

Evie felt awful. Not only was she in Lottie Dean's bad books, but her beautiful, lucky party dress was covered in crumbs and squash. *And still no one is speaking to me*, she reminded herself.

Miss Connie squeezed her hand, then started to wipe away the butter that was smeared all over the butterfly belt.

Evie felt hot tears filling her eyes once more and, this time, she didn't have the strength to hold them back. Then, lower lip trembling, she caught a glimpse of emerald green out of the corner of her watery eye.

'Beth!' she whispered in amazement. She was wearing the very same dress!

Evie fell silent. Beth had snubbed her too many times that week, and she wasn't going to risk it happening again. Besides, it looked as though Beth was scowling at her. Until, suddenly, her freckled face broke into a grin and she fell into a fit of giggles.

'Hey, I love your dress!' Beth said, running over to Evie and wrapping her up in a huge hug.

'You've got great taste!' joked Evie, who was thrilled to have her special friend back again. Miss Connie had got rid of some of the butter, so she brushed away the crumbs and knew that her mum could sort out any other damage. Having a friend to enjoy the disco with was a million times more important than a perfect-looking dress!

In the entrance to the studio, a flash of bright pink caught Evie's eye. True to form, Mrs Dean had come rushing to Lottie's rescue with another beautiful party outfit to replace the one that had been covered in crumbs. Evie looked down at her slightly grubby belt and realised that she really

STAR

didn't mind about it at all. She was just so pleased to have her friends back.

Beth grabbed Evie's hand and they ran towards the dance floor to find the rest of the gang. Meera taught her a funky routine and she laughed with Jess and Lauren at the boys' daft dancing. As she and Beth pulled cheesy grins for a photo, Evie realised that the worst night of her life had turned into the best.

Thank you, she thought, sending a wish to the marvellous, magical friend who lay hidden under her pillow.

Dancing Diva

Be a ballet babe with our guide to all the classic ballet positions you need to know!

First Position

Your arms should be curved naturally straight out in front of you, with your hands very softly cupped.

Second Position

Move your arms so that they are held out to the side at right angles to your body, making sure that your elbows are gently curved.

Third Position

Move one of your arms in front of your body, and leave the other as it is in second position.

Fourth Position

Keep one arm the same as in second position and raise the other one up above your head.

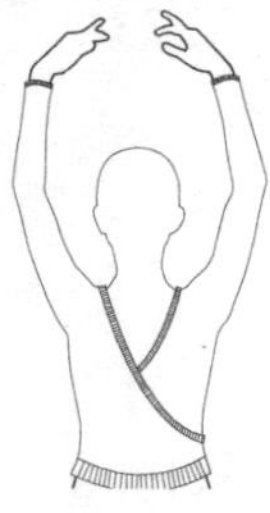

Fifth Position

Put both arms above your head with your elbows gently curved and hands slightly apart.

Find more cool ballet moves in the next From Your Diary With Love book.

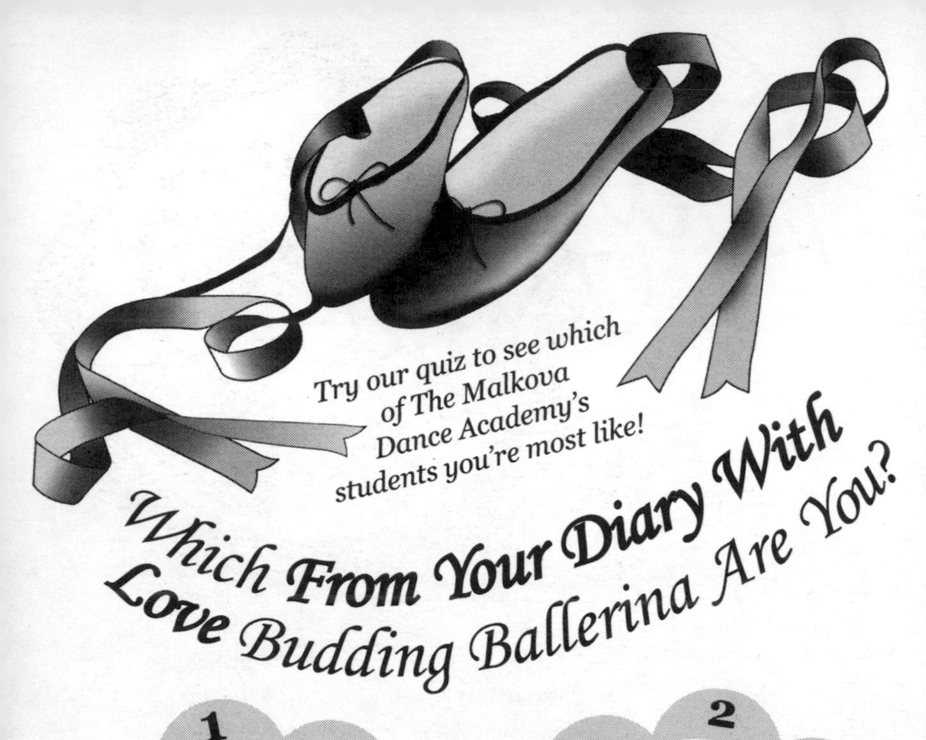

Try our quiz to see which of The Malkova Dance Academy's students you're most like!

Which *From Your Diary With Love* Budding Ballerina Are You?

1

The hardest thing about dancing is . . .

a. Getting the moves totally right

b. Having to deal with other people

c. Not falling over on stage!

2

When you're not dancing, you're . . .

a. Hanging out with your best mates

b. Shopping – you have to look good all the time

c. On the footy pitch – you just can't sit still!

3

You'd love to be famous for your . . .

a. Amazing dancing!

b. Gorgeous good looks!

c. Top talents!

4

Which word best describes your dancing style . . .

a. Graceful

b. Dramatic

c. Funky

5

You love to dance in . . .

a. Tutus and tiaras

b. The best costume in the show

c. Whatever's comfy

Mostly **As**

Lottie

Just like Lottie, you're a dancing diva who has to be noticed! You love being on stage, stealing the show and showing everyone how awesome you are!

Mostly **Bs**

Evie

You and Evie are like peas in a pod! You both love dancing, dreaming and doing everything as well as you can! One day you could both be very famous ballerinas!

Mostly **Cs**

Lauren

You and Lauren could be best buds! You both hate being bored and are just as happy doing *pliés* at the *barre* as playing footy on the pitch! You go, girl!

6

Your fave kind of dancing is . . .

a. Any, you just love to dance!

b. Ballet, especially when you're the female lead

c. Modern, you wanna be a disco diva!

Heavenly Hair

Look the part with this dance-friendly hairstyle!

What you will need:

- 2 elastic hairbands
- 3 coloured ribbons – make sure they are quite thin and long!
- Hairbrush

What to do:

1. Start by brushing your hair to get rid of any knots

2. Next, tie the three coloured ribbons on to the elastic hairband

3. Now, make a ponytail and secure it with that elastic band

4. Divide your ponytail into three equal sections (just like you would when you plait your hair), then put one ribbon into each of the sections

5. Now plait your hair, keeping a ribbon in each section. The ribbons should add some colour to your plait

6. When you get to the end of your hair secure it with the other elastic hairband, leaving the ends of the ribbon dangling. You can always get a grown-up to cut the ribbons to the same length as your hair if they look super-long

7. Ta da – a gorgeous hairstyle perfect for on and off stage!

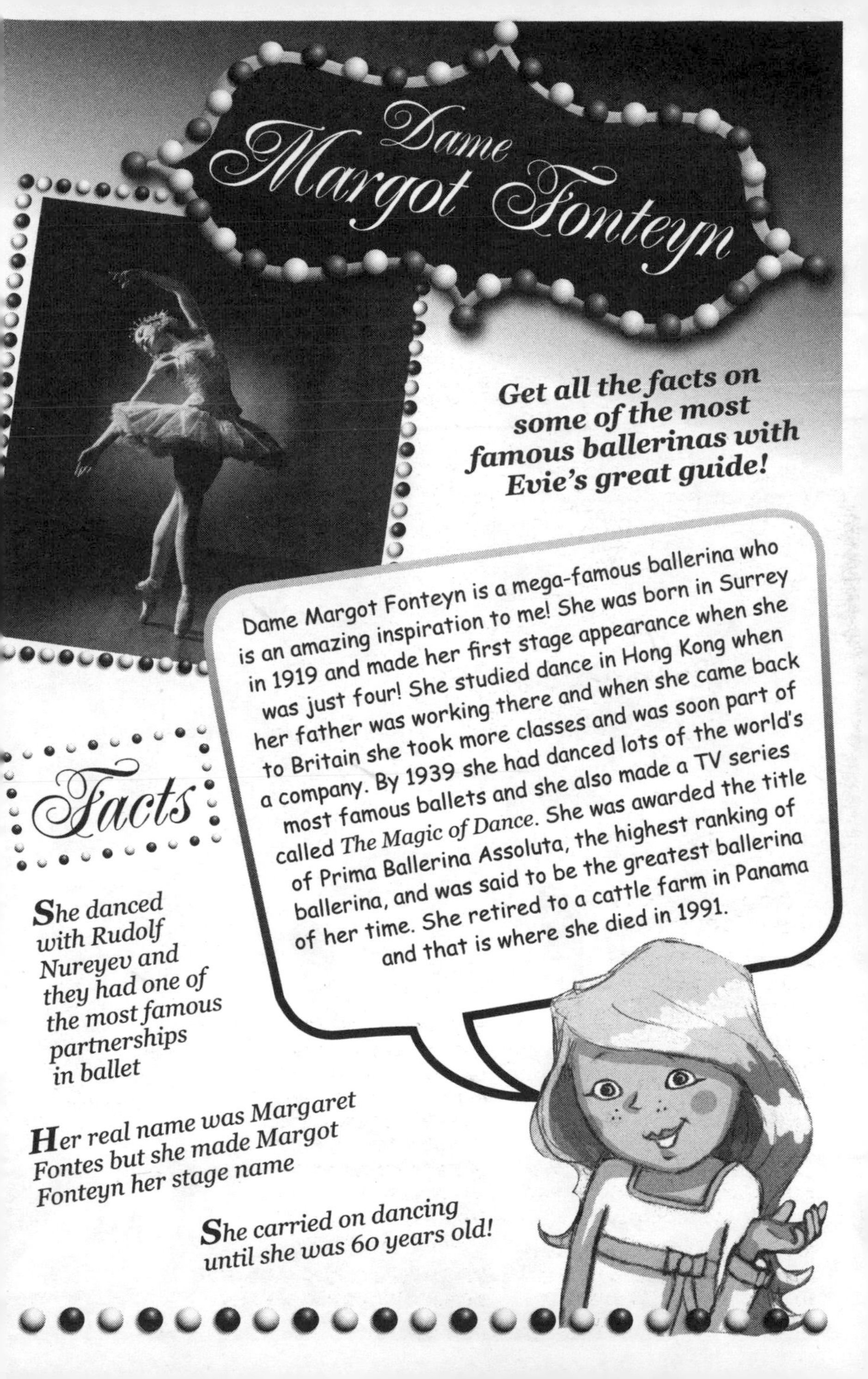

Dame
Margot Fonteyn
Get all the facts on some of the most famous ballerinas with Evie's great guide!
Dame Margot Fonteyn is a mega-famous ballerina who is an amazing inspiration to me! She was born in Surrey in 1919 and made her first stage appearance when she was just four! She studied dance in Hong Kong when her father was working there and when she came back to Britain she took more classes and was soon part of a company. By 1939 she had danced lots of the world's most famous ballets and she also made a TV series called *The Magic of Dance*. She was awarded the title of Prima Ballerina Assoluta, the highest ranking of ballerina, and was said to be the greatest ballerina of her time. She retired to a cattle farm in Panama and that is where she died in 1991.
Facts
She danced with Rudolf Nureyev and they had one of the most famous partnerships in ballet
Her real name was Margaret Fontes but she made Margot Fonteyn her stage name
She carried on dancing until she was 60 years old!

True or False Quiz
Think you can remember everything about this brill book? Try our quiz to see how you score!
1
Meera's parents want her to be a doctor
True or False
2
The only boy at The Malkova Dance Academy is Matt Shanklin
True or False
3
Evie falls in love with a pink dress
True or False
4
Evie and Beth fall out over the secret diary
True or False
5
Evie and Lottie both end up with soup all over their dresses
True or False
6
Evie spots Mrs Swann having tea with Mrs Volkov
True or False
7
Jess wins the poster competition
True or False
Answers
1 False; 2 True; 3 False; 4 True; 5 False; 6 True; 7 False

Can't wait for the next book in the series? Here's a sneak preview of

Chapter One

Sleepover Secrets

'Pass the popcorn, Evie,' said Hannah, Evie's oldest friend, as the pair snuggled up under a cosy quilt to watch *Ballet Stars* on DVD for the millionth time.

'Watch it!' squealed Hannah, as a piece of popcorn bounced off her head and wedged itself down the side of the sofa. Evie burst into giggles at her friend's horrified face.

'Right, you asked for it!' said Hannah, launching a shower of popcorn on to Evie's head.

Soon, the pair were in fits of laughter, their legs tangled up in the quilt as they wriggled about on the sofa.

Red-cheeked, Evie beamed from ear to ear. She was beginning to like her new home in Crossacre, but there was something special about having Hannah to stay. They had stuck together since they first met aged three, a pair of chubby-cheeked tots who held hands and skipped together in their first ballet class. Seven years later, they still shared everything: clothes, gossip, secrets and, of course, their passion for dance.

'We'd better clean this up,' said Evie, gathering the bits of popcorn from the sofa.

'Ooh, I love this bit,' sighed Hannah, as Darcey Bussell pirouetted across the screen in a snow-white tutu. The pair had watched this part of *Swan Lake* so many times that they knew the routine off by heart.

'I wish I could dance *en pointe* like that,' said Evie, her voice full of admiration. 'Mrs Swann said I might be able to give it a go in a couple of years.'

'Brilliant!' said Hannah, hugging Evie and humming along to the famous ballet music softly.

'Oi, oi, oi!' boomed a loud voice as the bright

sitting room light glared on. It was Evie's big brother Charlie, swiftly followed by her dad and little brother Josh, who grabbed the remote control from the coffee table. The beautiful ballerina suddenly disappeared from the screen, and was replaced by a roaring football crowd.

'Football?!' the girls cried together, pulling disgusted faces.

'I'm sorry, girls,' said Mr Denham with a shrug. 'But it's the big match and we just have to watch it, I'm afraid. Millchester United don't get through to the second round of the FA Cup every day, you know!'

'Yeah, we *have* to watch it,' added Josh, handing the newly ejected DVD to Evie with a smug grin.

'There's no point in arguing,' Evie explained to Hannah. 'We'll never win when there's football involved. Come on, let's go upstairs. At least there aren't any boys up there.'

The girls stomped up to Evie's bedroom in their fluffy slippers and pyjamas, stopping to poke their tongues out at Josh and Charlie from halfway up the stairs.

Evie and Hannah jumped into the huge makeshift bed they had made on the floor earlier that day. They had piled Evie's polka-dot duvet and pillows on to a spare mattress, then added every blanket and cushion that they could find to make a cosy nest that was big enough for both of them to sleep in. The two friends soon settled down into their old sleepover routine of swapping gossip.

'Did I tell you about Mr Humphries and the frog?' Hannah whispered to Evie.

'Oh, please tell me!' said Evie, keen to catch up on the news from her old school.

'We were in the middle of assembly when suddenly Mr Humphries let out a huge yelp,' said

Hannah, her eyes sparkling in the half-light. 'He started to leap around the hall with a frog on his head! It must have jumped in through the window. I wish you'd been there, Evie.' The girls rolled around with laughter. 'Now, whenever Mr Humphries walks past, Jamie Maxwell croaks!'

Evie loved hearing stories from her old school back in London, but when she realised that she couldn't even picture Jamie Maxwell's face, she felt a little sad. *I guess I am drifting away from my old life*, she thought. *But at least I'll always have Hannah as my friend*.

The girls stayed up talking for hours, comparing stories from their dance lessons and tales of annoying little brothers. As Evie rearranged the pillows under her head, she felt something solid shift between them. Feeling around the layers of bedding, her hand began to tingle. *My diary!* she realised, running her fingers over its soft, velvet cover. *I can't believe I forgot to tell Hannah!*

Whenever Evie had a problem, her diary came up with the perfect advice. All she had to do was write about it and wait for her diary to pen a reply. Then Evie remembered her diary's request that she keep it a secret.

Please, Evie, keep me hidden,
For if anyone finds out,
These words will fade, and I'll be gone.
Of this there is no doubt.

But Evie couldn't keep the excitement to herself. She could just imagine how thrilled Hannah would be about it all. Surely it was impossible to keep a secret like that from her very best friend?

Just as Evie opened her mouth to reveal all,

Hannah sighed contentedly and rolled over to face the wall.

Realising that Hannah was asleep, Evie took a deep breath. That had been close.